Help for the Trolley

An Ogunquit Tale

By Judith Johnson-Siebold

Illustrated by Jeff Boyer

A trolley named Dolly zipped all around town.
She carried the people both up hill and down.
She drove through Ogunquit,
a village in Maine.
She ran in the fog, in the sun and the rain.

"I'm tired," she said to herself one fine day.
"I need some time off
to just go out and play.
I drive in the springtime. I drive in the fall.
I drive in the summer with no rest at all."

"My gears are all weary;
my springs are all sprung.
My tires are tired; my engine's not young.
My seats are all sagging; I don't feel my best.
It's clearly important I have a long rest."

She crept down a side street
that led to the sea and said to herself,
"I just want to be free.
I want to have freedom to go out and play.
I want to be able to stay out all day."

When she reached the ocean she drove on the beach
and tried to catch seagulls that ran beyond reach.
She zoomed down the beach just as fast as she could.
She breathed in the sea breeze and thought,
"That smells good."

She picked up some seashells to put in a box
along with some driftwood,
some sea glass and rocks.
She went to the shoreline and feeling quite brave,
she drove in the water and jumped each tall wave.

Then after a while she sat on the beach
and made a sandcastle
the waves couldn't reach.
A black and white seagull let out a shrill cry.
It ran down the beach and then started to fly.

Clouds suddenly covered the sun like a frown,
and then a thought hit her:
"I've let people down.
They needed a trolley; they've waited all day.
They're counting on me, while I sit here and play."

She rushed off the beach and back on the road.
Her heart felt as though it was pulling a load.
She needed a nap, and she wanted to sleep
but knew that she had
a great promise to keep.

So she asked her sisters and brothers at home,
"I need you to help. I can't do this alone."
Her sisters and brothers were pleased to be asked.
They knew how to drive —
not too slow, not too fast.

When people now go to Ogunquit in Maine
they see all the trolleys,
each one with a name —
Dolly and Holly and Jolly and Lolly,
Molly and Polly and Rolly and Wally.

They drive through the streets
with both skill and with care,
and all of the people are glad they are there.
They drive in the rain, in the fog and the sun,
and they help each other take time out for fun.

SHIRES ♦ PRESS

4869 Main Street
P.O. Box 2200
Manchester Center, VT 05255
www.northshire.com

© 2015 by Judith Johnson-Siebold
Illustrations © 2015 by Jeff Boyer

ISBN 978-1-60571-273-4

NORTHSHIRE BOOKSTORE

Building Community, One Book at a Tim
A family-owned, independent booksto
in Manchester Ctr., VT, since 19
and Saratoga Springs, NY since 20
We are committed to excellence in booksellin
The Northshire Bookstore's mission is to serve as a resour
for information, ideas, and entertainment while honori
the needs of customers, staff, and communi

Printed in the United States of Ameri

CPSIA information can be obtained at www.ICGtesting.com
Printed in the USA
BVIW12n2313250716
456839BV00001B/1